CANCELLED

D0257208

THE LAST
BOOK
BEFORE
BEDTIME

For my husband Sjoerd, who is snuggly and wonderful
N.O. x

First published 2016 by Nosy Crow Ltd.
The Crow's Nest, 10a Lant Street,
London SE1 1QR
www.nosycrow.com

ISBN 978 0 85763 428 3 (HB)
ISBN 978 0 85763 598 3 (PB)

Nosy Crow and associated logos are trademarks and/or registered trademarks of Nosy Crow Ltd.

Text and illustrations © Nicola O'Byrne 2016

The right of Nicola O'Byrne to be identified as the author and illustrator of this work has been asserted.

A CIP catalogue record for this book is available from the British Library.

Printed in China by Imago

Papers used by Nosy Crow are made from wood grown in sustainable forests.

1 3 5 7 9 8 6 4 2 (HB)
3 5 7 9 8 6 4 2 (PB)

THE LAST
BOOK
BEFORE
BEDTIME

NICOLA
O'BYRNE

523 180 93 X

A T THE END OF A DAY that's been filled with lovely things that ping and beep and buzz and glow, there's nothing better than one last-book-before-bed.

You could say it's the most important story of the whole day. But which story will it be?

Um . . . hello? Three Little Pigs, can you hear me?

I SAID . . . what could the last-book-before-bed possibly be?!

Please excuse us, we seem to be having some technical difficulties.

But I'm in the middle of a game!

The last-book-before-bed? Oooh, that sounds interesting!

Um . . . excuse me, Three Little Pigs.
It's time for the story to start **NOW.**
We have a really sleepy reader here,
and we need a bedtime story!

Is there
time for cake
first?

Get ready, Little Pigs, or we'll read something else!
Come on, let's get this show on the road . . .

Right. At last, we can get started.

ONCE UPON A TIME, there were Three Little Pigs. When they were all grown-up, their mother sent them out into the world to seek their fortunes, but first she kissed them on their piggy noses and said, "Work hard, and remember – beware of the

BIG BAD WOLF!"

Home

The big wide world

The Three Little Pigs soon found a meadow where the flowers smelled so lovely, and the river bubbled so cheerfully, that the First Little Pig declared, "This meadow is perfect! I shall build my house right here, and I shall make it out of straw!"

Well, we all know how THAT'S going to turn out.

But before the First Little Pig could even start
building his house, there was a rather pink interruption.

It was Cinderella.

If this is the last storybook before bedtime, you really want a PRINCESS story. My book has romance, an evil stepmother and everyone knows princess stories are made into films and toys. No one's going to want to watch a film with you pork chops in it.

Well, you're here now Cinderella. Let's see what happens . . .

Once upon a time, there was a beautiful maiden who lived with her **evil** stepmother and two **ugly** sisters. The maiden was sweet and lovely but her family was mean.

They made her sleep by the fireplace and, because she was always covered in cinders, they called her Cinderella.

One day, an invitation arrived from the Royal Palace.
The Prince was holding a grand ball and everyone
was invited! Everyone, that is, except Cinderella.
Her **evil** stepmother would **NOT** let her go.

Settle down, Little Pigs. You three can be the **evil** stepmother
and the **ugly** stepsisters. Right, Pigs! Get your dresses on!

As the Three Little Pigs – sorry, the **evil** stepmother and the **ugly** stepsisters – left the house, Cinderella began to cry, for she desperately wanted to go to the ball, too.

Suddenly, there was a puff of magic and a fairy appeared!

We shall go to the ball!

I said . . . A FAIRY APPEARED!

Well, this is embarrassing.

It usually works. Let's try again.

Suddenly, there was a **PUFF of MAGIC** and . . .

. . . Little Red Riding Hood and the Big Bad Wolf appeared?! That's a surprise!

Listen, the Fairy Godmother can't make it. Ignore all this fancy princess stuff – the last storybook should be exciting, and full of action and danger. I'm way more interesting than the "Cinderella" story.

Did I miss anything?

Well, now that you're both here,
let's get back to the story.

Well, I think
"Cinderella" is
an exciting story.
So there.

Oh.
It's you.

Does this mean
we have to
start again?

But we're
nearly at the
cake part of
the story.

Everyone settle down! Let's try again.
Cinderella, you can be Little Red's mother. Pig number two,
you're the granny. And Wolf, you're not in this bit.

ONCE UPON A TIME, there was a little girl whose cloak had a beautiful red hood, so everyone called her Little Red Riding Hood. One day, her mother said to her, "Could you take this picnic basket to your granny? But don't stray from the forest path and remember – beware of the

BIG BAD WOLF!"

It's boring being the mum.

Little Red Riding Hood was skipping along,
when who should she meet but the Big Bad Wolf?
"Good morning, Little Red Riding Hood," he said.
"Where are you off to so early and all by yourself?"

"I'm off to see my poor, sick granny and take her some of my mother's elderflower cordial and cake," replied Little Red Riding Hood.

Everyone, quiet down! You're ruining the story! And be careful! Don't you know that books are only made of paper?!

THIS IS RIDICULOUS! If I can't be the star of the story, then NOBODY can! I'm going to pull this book to pieces!

I was promised cake!

Huh! Two can play at that game, Cinderella. You can't always be the centre of attention!

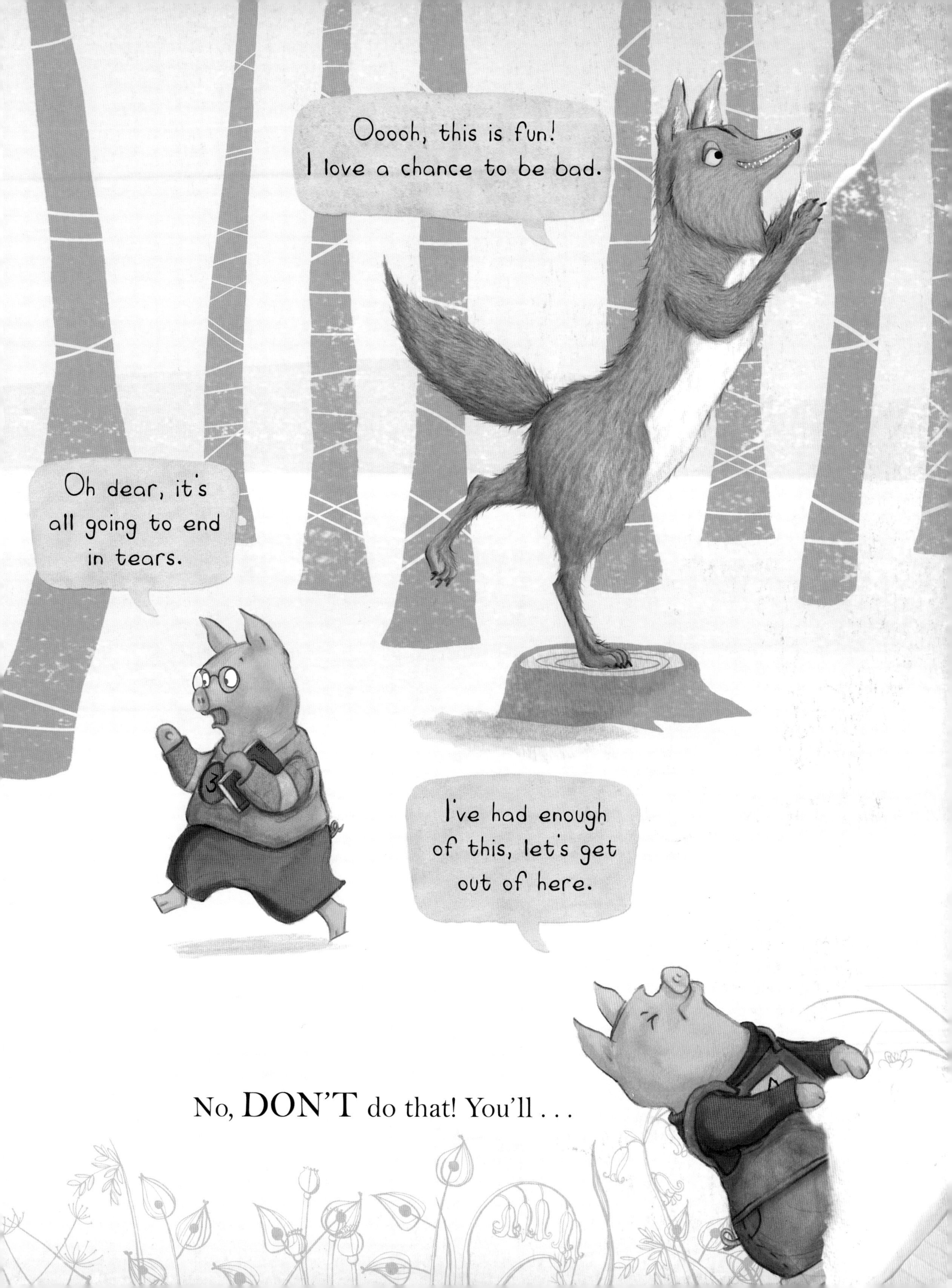

No, **DON'T** do that! You'll . . .

. . . rip

the

book!

OH NO! The book's in pieces!

And now it's bedtime and we have **NO** story.

Whatever are we going to do?

O NCE UPON A TIME, there were Three Little Pigs.
They were hard-working and resourceful,
and lived in a beautiful brick house in a lovely location.
On this particular day, they were hosting tea and cake
for their friends, Little Red Riding Hood and Cinderella.

Just then, Little Red Riding Hood arrived.

"Cinderella's just texted me," she said.

"She's not feeling well and won't be able to come to tea."

"Then we shall go to her!" cried the Third Little Pig,
who was not only handsome but kind and good.
So they packed up all of the lovely food and drink
and set off for Cinderella's house.

The path to Cinderella's house
wound through a deep, dark forest
and who should they meet there
but the Big Bad Wolf?

The Three Little Pigs and Little Red Riding Hood were afraid of wolves and decided not to stop and talk, but this wolf saw the picnic basket and guessed where they were going.

"I'm going to sneak to Cinderella's house first," thought the wolf, "and when they arrive, I'll **gobble** them up!"

When the Three Little Pigs and Little Red Riding Hood arrived at Cinderella's house, they found SOMEONE in bed – SOMEONE who was wearing Cinderella's favourite pink scarf.

"What big **eyes** you have," said Little Red Riding Hood.

"All the better to see you with!" said the SOMEONE.

"What big **ears** you have," said Little Red Riding Hood.

"All the better to hear you with," said the SOMEONE.

The Third Little Pig looked at the SOMEONE very carefully.

"What big **teeth** you have," said the Third Little Pig.

"All the better to . . .

... EAT
YOU WITH!"

shouted the Big Bad Wolf,
and he leapt out of bed.

But the Third Little Pig
knew exactly what
to do next . . .

. . . he leapt forward and wedged a large slice
of cake firmly into the Wolf's huge, toothy mouth.
"IT'S SO DELICIOUS!" cried the Wolf.
"Even tastier than little pigs or little girls!"

The First Little Pig then let
Cinderella out of the cupboard,
where she promptly fell in love
with him.

Is this the romantic
bit? But I'm a pig!

Well,
nobody's
perfect.

But they didn't kiss
because this isn't
THAT kind of story.

And they all lived happily ever after.

Well done, team! You did a great job in the end!

That was just what a last-book-before-bed should be.

Are **you** still awake?! Oh, no!

But we've run out of pages!

We're going to need another book!

Which book are **you** going to choose?